Andrea Hofer Proudfoot

Child's Christ-tales

Souvenir Edition

Andrea Hofer Proudfoot

Child's Christ-tales
Souvenir Edition

ISBN/EAN: 9783337120160

Printed in Europe, USA, Canada, Australia, Japan

Cover: Foto ©Andreas Hilbeck / pixelio.de

More available books at **www.hansebooks.com**

CHILD'S CHRIST-TALES

BY

ANDREA HOFER PROUDFOOT

Illustrated

*EIGHT THOUSAND
SOUVENIR EDITION*

CHICAGO
PUBLISHED BY THE AUTHOR
1400 AUDITORIUM

CONTENTS

CONTENTS — *Continued.*

CHRIST-CHILD
"The Father and I are one"
(*F. Ittenbach*)

MADONNA SAINT SISTINE
(*Raphael*)

THERE was once a promise made to all
the people of the world, and every one
was waiting and had been waiting long for it
to be kept.

No one could remember who had made the
promise, but the little children were told that
it was made by a great King who knew everything that had ever happened, and all things
that would ever be.

And this was the promise:

A wonderful flower was to grow in a certain
garden that would bring to the one who owned
the garden all the good things in the world.

Every one waited and waited for the flower
to come. Years and years they had waited —
summer after summer; each new little boy and
girl that came into the world was told of the
great promise, and among the very first things
they did was to go about seeking the flower
and asking questions about it.

But no one could tell them anything except to repeat the promise that a beautiful gift-plant would some day grow upon the earth, which only people with loving hearts could see, and they should be greatly blessed.

Every one in the whole world went about looking for this flower, even though they did a great deal of work, and thought of other things, yet they never quite forgot the wonderful promise.

Many of them prepared the soil and made beautiful gardens to receive it. Some sought far and wide for rare seeds and bulbs which they planted and watered, but only such plants grew as every one had seen before, and so they still waited and searched.

Many others wished and wished, and some prayed and prayed, but the precious seed did not come.

The rich men of the land had great parks laid out; the ground was tilled and everything kept ready for the plant to find root. Many gardeners and watchers were hired to stay there and watch for this wondrous flower and guard it — but it did not come.

Yet no one ever doubted the promise, for every one wished very much to have all the good things which were to come with this flower.

Among all these people there was one very kind woman, who did many good deeds. She loved and cared for little children who had no one to help them. One night when she came home from her work what did she see in a little broken flower-pot that stood in her window?

A tiny plant which she had never noticed before! She watered it and it grew and grew, and she learned to love it.

One day while she was looking at the tiny plant she remembered the promise, and said quietly to herself: "Can it be that this is the beautiful flower the whole world is waiting for! I think it is, for it has made me so happy."

And it was the flower.

She knew the promise had come because it made her so happy.

Every one, far and near, came to see it; and they begged pieces and seeds to plant. And though the good woman gave of her plant, it grew larger and larger, and she became happier and happier.

One day it blossomed wide and beautiful.

The rich men who had made great parks and gardens for the flower would not believe the woman had received the real promised plant. They shook their heads and laughed at it all, and went on seeking after other seeds and plants.

But the people who believed because they saw how happy it made the woman to whom the flower came, brought rich gifts to her and begged for the seed, and they took it home and planted it everywhere, that the whole world might be filled with joy and peace.

SAINT JOHN THE BAPTIST
(Paul Baudry)

SO many things that children love to hear happened very long ago. This story of David and John is an old, old story, and we only remember it through songs and legends that have been told and related by the great story-tellers and singers of years long past.

David was a shepherd boy.

He tended sheep in his father's pastures, and in the long days of summer he watched the young lambs play round the mother sheep. He sang to them and played upon his harp — for he loved them; and he loved the warm sunshine and the green meadow with all his heart.

All of David's people owned pastures and raised sheep. They were people who loved their country and its people with a deep love, and they had taught their children to love God most of all.

So David, while he led his sheep through the green pastures and beside the still waters, thought many thoughts about these things.

The nation to which David belonged had

received a promise in the beginning, that there would some day come to it a King to rule and bless its people.

This King was to come from God, and the whole world would bow down before him.

David, when he was out in the sweet fields, would sing of this promise, and with his fingers touch the harp in time with his voice, until, it is said, the flock gathered round him and listened.

And there, amid his sheep, he learned to love the King who was to come; and deep down in his heart he believed that the promise would surely be fulfilled.

And it was.

There was another youth called John, who received the same promise that came to David. He lived a long time after David, but the great King had not yet come.

Still no one had ever doubted the promise, for the nation was very unhappy and had had great troubles, and was looking and longing for

SAINT JOHN, CHRIST-CHILD AND LAMB
(*Murillo*

a wise ruler to help them. They all thought
this promised King would come in great glory
and sit upon a throne, with beauty and grandeur all about him.

As a boy John passed his days under the
sky in the fields and woods. He ate fruits and
honey, and had never seen a city or many
people.

His father and mother had told him many
times of the promised King, but John knew
very little of what thrones and rulers meant,
and even less of what the world was thinking.
But he knew that such a man as would come
from God must be a perfect man, who would
know and do only the good.

John left the wilderness and woods when he
became older and went out among the people;
When he saw how strange were their thoughts
of this man of God, who was to come, he told
them they must look for their King as holy
and pure, not as a worldly king.

God put it into his heart to make clear to

these people, and tell them of this King who was to come quickly.

Many men and women followed after John wherever he went, for they loved to hear his words. And great numbers believed, watching every day more eagerly than before for this King, the Son of God, who was to come and be their ruler.

THE ANNUNCIATION
(*Murillo*)

SUPPOSING an angel should speak to you! Deep in your ear you should hear it, and deep in your heart you should believe its words; and when you turned about there was no angel there!

What would you think?

No one could make you believe it never happened; and would you not watch and wait for its promises to come true?

This is just what happened to a beautiful young woman the world has always called Mary.

She sat one morning with her hands filled with flowers, and her eyes far away out upon the field. She was most happy, because of the beauty all about her and because of the loving deeds done.

Suddenly, from above and below, and all about, there began to pour a light which almost blinded her eyes, and as she peered into it, she heard a clear, still voice from out its deepest brightness, saying:

"Joy to thee, Mary! God is with thee; blessed art thou among women! Mary, God loveth thee; and behold, thou shalt bring forth a son, and call his name Jesus. He shall be great; he shall be called the Son of God; he shall be placed upon the throne, and of his kingdom there shall be no end."

And the angel ceased.

As she listened and looked, she knew it must be an angel. Its form became brighter and brighter, even brighter than the light, and deep, deep eyes looked down upon her and into her eyes, until they, too, streamed with light.

And the angel left her.

She sat long and dreamed it all over and over. The flowers had dropped from her hands and the light of her eyes streamed out toward the blue sky.

No one came near her, and for a long time

she was all alone, with only the angel's promise to dream about.

Think what a sweet promise it was—that a holy child should come to her and lie close to her breast, and look up into her face and tell her with its smiles of God and heaven.

Every baby can tell to every one of us the same sweet story, if we will only believe and watch for the promises of the angel who always tells us of its coming.

THE HOLY NIGHT
(*Feuerstein*)

THE great King did come upon the earth, to all the waiting people.

The world had grown so tired that it was beginning to forget the promise, and just when they least thought of it, lo! it came true.

On the first Christmas morning, before the light had come, the great King came upon the earth.

It was the same King that David had sung of, and the same King that John had told about! The same King the world had waited for!

And this was how it came about.

Shepherds were watching their flocks by night, and they dreamed that their King had come. They awoke suddenly and saw a bright light and they heard voices which told them to follow the beautiful star which was standing high in the heavens, for its light would lead them to where the King was.

They arose in the night and followed the star a long way, when suddenly it stopped and hung over the very place where they were to find their King. And they went in; and lo! they found that their great King was only a tiny babe; its throne was its mother's knee, and its palace was a manger.

Wonderful stories are told by those who came to the manger and found the little child. They saw a bright light above it, that lighted its face and all about it. And they brought gifts and laid them at the mother's feet.

They called the babe their King, for they believed it was the child of God. The shepherds went out among the people full of joy and thanks, and told all they met of the babe that was born to be their King.

"The little Christ-Child lay in a manger bed because there was no room at the inns. A great many people journeyed toward the little town of Bethlehem that long-ago time, before the first Christmas day; and when the mother

THE ARRIVAL AT BETHLEHEM
(*L. Olivier Merson*)

and father reached their journey's end at
nightfall, every inn was filled with travelers
—no bed for the sweet young mother, so
weary after her long day's journey. Bethlehem was filled. There were not houses
enough for so many people. A warm shelter
and a soft bed on the manger hay of the great
hillside stable was all the good inn keeper
could give; and there with the kind-eyed oxen
and sheep all about, and the angels hovering
o'er, the beautiful Christ-Child lay asleep in
the manger. A great star shone overhead,
and the angels sang softly. Thus it was the
Christ-Child brought peace and joy to the
world, even though he lay upon a manger bed
when he came to Bethlehem on that Christmas
night, so long ago."

MADONNA AND CHILD
(*C. Muller*)

O F all the beautiful mothers, think how beautiful must be the mother of a King!

If you and I love the king-child Jesus, how must his own mother have loved him! Think how happy the sweet mother Mary was when the perfect little boy-king, which she had been promised, really lay in her lap where she could touch him.

As she hung over him and his shining eyes looked into hers, she watched him, listening for the signs by which she would surely know he was the King.

And as over the face of the babe there crept smiles, no one knew what those smiles meant except the mother; for she knew that the smiles of her child would bring peace to the world.

The angel had promised that he should be great; but as she looked down upon him, her eyes saw that he was tiny indeed, yet her heart knew that he was great, both in loveliness and love.

The angel had promised her that he should come to her as the true child of God; and when the beautiful mother saw the shining, living child, full of holy life, she knew that only the great Father could have given him to her.

The angel had promised her that he should sit upon the throne and be a great King and rule all the world; and although he was born in the cattle stall, the mother knew that every loving creature that might look upon him would be only too glad to call so pure a child their master, and even King.

And she made of her heart a treasure box, and kept all these sweet promises within her.

Over and over, as she sang sweet words to her golden child, she thought of these promises of the angel, and knew that some day the world, too, would know them, if only she, his mother, would never forget.

MADONNA AND CHILD
(*Dagnan Bouveret*)

The mother never did forget, for we have all heard, ever since we were little babes, of this precious King, and of his beautiful heart-kingdom, and of the children of God that live therein.

Blessed be the mother that never forgot.

LONG, long ago—so long that even the old
gray hills have forgotten—the beautiful
stars in the sky used to sing together very early
every morning, before any of the little people
of the world were up. Their songs were made
of light, and were so clear and strong that
the whole heaven would shine when they
sang.

One morning, as the stars sang and listened to each other, they heard a beautiful
music coming swiftly toward them. It was
so much louder and sweeter than their own
that they all stopped and listened and wondered. It came from far above them, from
out the very deepest blue of the sky. It was
a new star, and it sang an entirely new song
that no one had ever heard before.

"Hark, hark!" the stars cried. "Let us
hear what it is saying."

And the beautiful star sang it over and over

again, and its song told of a lovely babe that had come on earth — a babe so beautiful that it was the joy of the whole world. Yes, so beautiful that when you looked at it you saw real light streaming from its face.

Every little child in the world has light in its face if we but know how to see it; but this little one had so very much that its mother wondered as she looked down upon her lap and saw it there. And there were shepherds there to look at the babe, and many other people saw it and could not understand.

But the one beautiful star knew — yes it knew all about it; and what do you think it knew? Why, that this child was God's own child, and was so good and loving that the whole world when it heard of it would want to know how to be so, too.

This one beautiful star traveled on and on, telling all the way what it knew of the child, and its light fairly danced through the sky, and hung over the very place where the little one lay.

All the other stars in the heavens were puzzled. They heard the song of the wonderful star that had come such a long, long way, and saw its brightness.

The words of its song were, "A loving child, a loving child is on the earth."

And as they listened these stars all looked down to find the child, but they could not see so far. And the strangest part of it all was, they could not sing their old songs any longer, the sweet new one was so much more beautiful, and so they sang that: "A loving child, a loving child is on the earth."

It is said that although they did not find the beautiful babe of which the great star sang, they are still seeking and listening and waiting. Every quiet evening they look down upon each little child, right down into each little heart, and ask, "Is this the child that is really loving?" They peep out of the sky just as the dear little babes are being tucked into bed, and down they peer, right into the windows.

That is why the stars come just at bed-time, for then they know where they can find the loving child. It is in its dear mother's lap, the light is shining in its face most of all, for it laughs up into the sweet eyes, and love seems all over everything. The stars know, for they have watched for many long years, and some day they will surely be satisfied.

And when they do find a truly loving child, a child with a shining face, a trusting heart and gentle ways, they will shine out brightly and sing with joy over and over again, "A loving child, a loving child is on the earth;" and again the heavens will light up and the wise men come and the manger be filled with shining, and the whole world will listen over again, and remember about the wonderful child that was born and is come again.

THE MOTHER AND CHRIST-CHILD
(*C. Froschl*)

MAGI ON THEIR WAY TO **BETHLEHEM**

(*Portaels*)

AS we all know there were once three wise men who traveled over the sands of the East searching for a King.

Such a long, long stretch over the burning hot sands of the desert they came, with loving, humble hearts, with only a single star to guide them, and with feet so willing to follow, if only they might find this King, of which the heavens had told them, and for which they had hoped and prayed so long.

We all know that these wise men really did find their King, for we have heard over and over the whole story.

But did you ever think how far they came; how they knelt before a young child on its mother's lap within a stable, and were satisfied to call him King, and then went their way again with glad hearts, knowing they had seen the real child of God!

Do all wise men long, as these three did, to

see in the tender, gentle heart of the babe the real child of God.

Do they travel the world over to search and understand the hearts of children?

Do they bring lovingly their precious gifts to the little ones? For the King, you know, said, "If ye do it unto one of the least of these, ye do it unto me."

REPOSE IN EGYPT

(*L. Olivier Merson*)

IT is told that this King took a long journey when he was only a tiny babe.

The prince of this world heard from the shepherds how they followed the star and how they found the child with such light streaming from its face that surely it must be the new King sent from God, of whom David had sung and John had told, and for whom the whole world was waiting.

And the prince of this world trembled for he feared lest this infant grow up and be made king in his place, to sit on his throne and rule his people.

And he sent soldiers out over the land to find the child and take him away.

One still night an angel of the Lord told the mother of the king's thought, and asked that the child be taken quietly away until the prince should forget.

And Mary, the mother, told her dream to

25

Joseph, and Joseph brought a beast of burden before the morning light came, and put the mother upon it, and the little child in her arms. Then with the halter in his hand he started out on foot toward the south, to Egypt, for there the angels had told them the little child would be safe.

Before they reached the land of the great River Nile they must pass many long days plodding through the hot sand, and it would have been a weary journey had not so many wonders happened.

Poets who love the gentle-hearted babe, and sing almost as David sang, have told us of this long journey through the south. They say the light with which he was born never left his face, and it lighted their way. The palm-trees stooped to give them fruit to eat. All the dangers of the desert passed them by; dry rose-bushes bloomed anew and filled the wide bare land with perfume, and the mother put them in her baby's hands.

REPOSE IN EGYPT
(*Plockhurst*)

26

Again the poet tells of how they rested by
the wayside, and as the sun stole across the
sky, the leaves of the tree under which they
sat moved with the sun to shade the baby and
his two beloved ones. And its shadow rested
on them all day long to keep the spot cool
whereon they sat.

And soon they came to where a great
rock-hewn figure spread itself in the sand.
The people of this land of Egypt loved to cut
these wondrous figures from the stone and
worship them.

Joseph led the beast up to the place and it
was evening, so they stopped to rest.

And on the breast of the great Sphinx the
mother leaned and the babe was in her arms.
Joseph kept watch by the slow fire and
strange things he thought as he watched
the smoke curl toward the soft southern sky.

Two years they wandered about the River
Nile. And there the child's soft feet took
their first steps which afterward led so many

friends into right paths; and there the baby's lips first learned to speak to the mother's eyes — those lips which since have spoken the sweetest words in all the world.

And this is the story of how the babe was saved from the cruel king.

And in two years, back they came to the little white-roofed city of Nazareth, and to the quiet home where Jesus grew to sweetest boyhood.

MADONNA AND CHILD
(*Ballheim*)

SEE the sweet baby look deep into the lily! He was such a lily himself, and had such a white, white heart with a golden center.

Tell me, have you ever thought how much the Christ-Child is like a lily?

Let me tell you how much. He came right from God's hand, just as a fresh spring lily does, and every word he spoke was sweet, even sweet as the lily smells; every one he touched was made happy, even as the lily makes us happy with its snowy brightness.

How well he understood what the lily meant by its whiteness and perfume! and what wonderful stories he told the world of his Father's love for the lily, for he dressed it in garments more beautiful than kings', even though it did no duties, except to give out sweetness and light.

We all love lilies and the Christ-Child, too, and in loving them we make them ours.

MADONNA OF THE WAVES
Detail
(*D. Maillart*)

ACROSS the blue water the sun was shining on the dear mother and her beautiful child. The waves sang sweet morning songs to them and over and over told their stories. From his childhood Jesus loved the water and loved the simple people who lived near the water.

Think what he must have heard when he listened to the waves telling in their deep voices the same stories over and over. He understood them, for you know when he was a man they listened to him, and stopped roaring when he spoke, and played round the boat in which he was riding, and gently splashed and sang.

Even the waves and winds obeyed him.

How he loved the water! Often, when the people crowded around him, he would go out in a boat with his own beloved waves about him and talk to those on the shore.

Did you ever hear the story how the waves helped him when he wished to go to his friends, and there was no way save over the water? They held up his feet as he stepped on them and were a strong path under him until he reached his beloved ones; and how they all marveled who saw him walk on the water, for though they had always lived near the water and were fishermen, yet they could not do such things.

The Christ-Child learned in the beginning the secret of the waves, and every thing in the world he knew and loved because his Father gave all things to him to help—and with all things he helped his beloved brothers. And his brothers were all men.

CHRIST PREACHING FROM A BOAT

(Hoffman)

ONCE there lived in Padua a boy,
    So calm and gentle, loving, meek and
        mild
The village wondered, and his folk
    Were puzzled at the goodness of the child.

Each day he lovelier grew, to both
    The eyes and hearts of all his mates in
        youth,
That they gave up the palm to this
    Gold-hearted, gentle lover of the truth.

How did he show his kindliness?
    Why friends, sweet friends, 'twas just in
        serving men;
In giving up his moments, pleasures, joys,
    His own self's claims to happiness, for them.

What did he do for them? what tasks?
    'Twere hard to tell. From early morn till
        late

He did such quiet, loving deeds—
　　That no one knew, and none would try to
　　　state.

He stopped in passing at each door
　　And watched the little ones with loving eyes;
He gave the mother comfort—helped
　　To tend the flock and still the infant's cries.

He calmed the anxious—sorrowing;
　　He labored with the poor and cheered the
　　　old;
He taught the sick that upward-looking
　　Which brings them joy and peace of heart
　　　untold.

He knelt oft by the sea and looked
　　Upon the vast, the throbbing heart
Of grandeur which the Lord had given
　　To the ocean's soul and to his own in part.

His lips sang songs to answer back
　　The melodies with which the great waves
　　　played

Up to his feet; and the songs were sweet
　　As if the earth and heaven prayed.

Oh his was a great heart, beloved ones.
　　When manhood set its crown upon his head,
He did such holy, gracious deeds to men,
　　And left his home and life for theirs instead.

That light and love which on us shines
　　Shone into him, this man of mother-heart;
Good things we only dream to do
　　He loved to do, and did the double part.

Once as he knelt beside the sea,
　　It seemed as though there came a holy child,
And nestling, stayed within his arms,
　　Close to his father-breast, so warm and mild.

The babe remained in his great arms,
　　And looked straight up into his earnest
　　　　face,
While lilies sprang beside his path,
　　And clouds of cherubs hovered o'er the
　　　　place.

And there beside him on the sand,
   The beaut'ous infant 'neath the lilies lay;
The great saint bent above its form,
   And watched and longed that it might ever
      stay.

The legend tells how the mother called,
   But the baby lay and waited long,—
For the loving heart within the saint
   Was sweet almost as the mother's song.

He felt the heart of Love had come,
   To beat within the bosom of a child,—
The babe, the Christ, uncalled had found
   His arms. He held it close and smiled.

Within his breast a rapture lived
   When long the vision fair had fled,
And glorious lights shone over all,
   That circled close and rested round his head.

Of Anthony, the saint, whose love
   For children taught the whole world how
      to love,

We tell this tale, and place his name
　All but one Holy name above.

We look upon his tender face,
　The painter taught us was his very own,
And love the Child his arms inclose,
　And say his Holy name with tenderer tone.

DID you ever see a little baby look away off with wonder in its face and its eyes shining? Did you ever see a baby smile in its sleep?

Poets and mothers love to tell wonder stories about what babes listen to when thus they smile and gaze far away.

The Christ mother and father had been promised that angels would come to their beautiful child and teach him all things and give him all the gifts of God. So that when his sweet eyes gazed away off, and he smiled at the blue sky and sunshine, and when he stretched his tiny hands to some one they could not see, the mother and father knew what it meant, and they, too, listened and looked.

Thus some music came into their own minds and hearts, and they understood these looks and smiles because they loved this won-

HOLY FAMILY
(*Müller*)

derful gift which came to them — this lovely child of God.

The Christ-Child learned to listen early to the music in his own heart, and he told it the best he could to all those around him.

Every little child hears this same angel music, for the heaven within us all is full of angels, singing forever of love and light.

DID you ever hear a story so sweet that you never can forget it?

Is there any story that has made you feel you would like to start right out and do something good or help some one?

Long years ago, when the Christ-Child first came upon the earth, stories were very few, and they were not in books as they are now. The only reading there was to be found was the wonderful sayings of the wise men, and the stories of the people who had lived before, which had been saved in writing. Think, if stories were few, how sweet they would be and how we would read them over and over!

Jesus as a child knew only these few stories. He heard them over and over, and as he grew older he searched them out for himself, for they were full of light and poetry, and many of them foretold the great things which were to happen.

SAINT JOSEPH AND CHRIST-CHILD
(*Murillo*)

39

Think what he must have felt when he read
that the Son of God was to come and save his
people from not only the wrongs which were
done toward them, but the very wrong that
was in their own hearts. As he read and
read, these wonderful thoughts would not
leave him. He began to see that these promises meant him, for he knew he understood
them as none of the friends about him did.
And as they grew clearer and clearer to him
he felt strong and great at heart and he could
hardly wait until he was grown, for he knew
that he could go out among the people and
show them what these writings meant.

He felt that he himself was indeed the Son
of God, and not only that, but he knew that
his Father was the great Father of all, and
therefore they need no longer go about in un-
happiness and sorrow.

Of course his friends were all surprised
when he began to show them these things,
and above all they believed when he proved

what he said by helping them to do good.

Best of all they loved to listen to him when
he told them sweet stories of his own, and thus
showed them what he meant. During all his
work among his friends he told them these
stories, and every story was so wonderful that
it made them go away and wish to start right
out and do good. Many did follow after him,
and they have written down these stories
which Jesus told for us all to read; and when
we read them we feel that they were told to
creep into our hearts, not alone, into our ears.

These stories come to us before we are tired
of listening, and that was when Jesus himself
read his stories, and he never forgot them and
was ever afterward so deeply moved by them
that he has moved the whole world to seek
what he found.

Are not those the sweetest stories in all the
world, which we can never forget because they
make us feel great and good and send us out
to help and do for others?

CHRIST IN THE TEMPLE

(*Hoffman*)

IN far-off Palestine, in years long past, the people of the villages and farms once a year went to the city of Jerusalem to celebrate the great feast.

They would start out in little parties from the different hamlets, and there would join them on the road, one by one, other travelers who were off on the same errand.

Great troops would enter the city together, and indeed it was much safer that they remain in close companies on the road.

And such happy chatting, visiting neighbors as they were, for it took many long days of travel to come, and many more before they reached home again.

Often whole families, mother, father, and children, went together, riding and walking, and resting by the way.

The boy Jesus, with Mary and Joseph, took this long journey, too, and many other little folks were along. Such a happy band as they were. The boys and girls would often rest themselves by mounting the camels and donkeys behind their mothers, and then be better ready for their long tramp.

They would stop by the way for their bread and meat and to sleep at night, so it took several days before they reached Jerusalem, where the feast was to be held.

Little Elizabeth, the neighbor's child, who lived in the house beyond that of Mary and Joseph, was a warm-hearted little girl of nine, and close companion of the boy Jesus. They would often stop and watch the long procession of friends and neighbors pass with their camels and bundles, and then, before their mothers and fathers, far to the front, were. lost to sight, they would run swiftly ahead and join them again.

And no one ever feared they would be lost, for all were going the same way and would guide the little ones.

43

At last they entered the great gates of Jerusalem, where the whole caravan parted to find
their resting places.

Mary and Joseph went to the house of some
friends, but Elizabeth pleaded so hard that
Jesus might go with her and her parents, that
it was finally allowed, for both the families
were to return together; and besides, his
mother was quite sure he could take care of
himself, for he was twelve years old.

The little boy and girl were very happy
together, and loved most of all to go to the
great temple where so many were always
coming and going.

On the morning of the day upon which
they were to return to their home the two
made one more visit, and looked once more
at the great walls and the wonderful crowd.

They sat down on a step to rest and Jesus
comforted Elizabeth, for she was very weary.
She leaned against him and he told her softly
of his Father who dwelt in heaven, and how

always he was rested at the thought of Him.

As he was teaching this little girl what he knew of his Father, a tall man in robes leaned over him and kindly said, "What is this, my lad?"

The sweet boy looked up into his face and said:

"I but told Elizabeth, who is weary, of the Father who rests and comforts us all. Do you know of Him?"

The man took him by the hand and said, "Tell me of Him."

And he led the children through the great temple door and far into the heart of the wonderful building where there sat five wise priests who taught the people of God.

And the man in the robes told them of the children and of their sayings, and the great priests asked what Jesus meant.

He answered their questions and they were astonished at his answers, for they saw that he truly believed that his Father was God, of

whom they taught but did not understand.
Jesus told them how this Father did all
things for him, and showed them how by
believing on Him and asking of Him we
received.

And many questions they asked him and he
answered them all clearly.

That day he was in the temple with the
great priests, and on the morrow they again
asked him of his Father, and his words made
them all wonder.

On the third day, as he sat in the midst
of the priests, Mary and Joseph found him.
They were greatly troubled, for they had
traveled a long way before they learned that
the two children were not in the party home-
ward bound. And Jesus told them how he
had taught the great priests of his Father in
heaven, which it was well that they should
know.

He left the five priests with loving adieux
and they were richly blessed with his wonder-

ful sayings. And the father and mother with the two little ones made haste to join their friends who had gone far ahead of them, and very soon the happy families were together again in Nazareth.

CHRIST-CHILD
(*Murillo*)

THE Christ stories in the Bible are nearly all about the man Jesus, and if we love to hear about him as a child, we must listen to the old, old stories which are seldom written, but told many times over and over, and especially in those countries where people read very little, but give all their best thought from mother to child by singing and story-telling.

When I was little and played about, we loved to play under grandmother's window; and all grandmother knew she had learned from her mother and grandmother in the far-away country where they teach by story and song. We used to love to play in clay and sand, and often made cosy little birds' nests of clay, and put eggs in them quite as natural and round as the real eggs. Then we would make the dear mother birds with widespread wings, and cover over the eggs with them;

and dear grandmother would stop her knitting and lean out the open window and look down on our work and say:

"Now, if you were little Christ children you could hatch the eggs and make them fly."

And with wonder we would hear her tell how the boy Jesus played with his companions one day, just as we were playing together then; and they made clay doves. When all were finished the Christ-Child clapped his hands and his birds flew into the air and were living things, just like all the real birds of the field.

And we all looked at grandma and wondered, just as his little companions must have wondered. And ever since this wonder has been in each heart: what was his power, his great power, which could bring life into a clay bird and make it fly? For grandmother's story must be true, and the same boy did so many strange things when he grew to be a man, and taught others to do them, too.

GUARDIAN ANGEL
(*Murillo*)

A LONG, long time ago, on the night just before Christmas, a little child, all alone, wandered in the streets of a large city.

There were a great many fathers and mothers hurrying home with bundles of presents for their little ones, and some rolled past in fine carriages, one after the other, bound for home to celebrate the happy time with their children.

This little child seemed to have no home, but just wandered up and down, looking into the windows and watching the lights. No one seemed to notice the little one except Jack Frost, who bit the bare toes and fingers, and the North Wind, who almost brought tears to the child's eyes with his blowing. It was cold, oh, very cold that night.

Up and down the street the little child passed, and the walks were all snowy and icy. The child had on neither shoes nor stockings;

but, though it was cold, the little one was glad, for it was Christmas eve, and the whole world seemed to be glad, too.

Everywhere the light was streaming out of the windows, and if one looked in, there could be seen the beautiful candles and the Christmas-trees. In some of the houses the trees were loaded with presents for the children, and in one place into which the little child looked the boys and girls were playing and skipping, and their merry laughter rang so loudly through the house, that it could be heard through the thick walls and doors out in the street.

The little child was glad with them, and clapped its hands and said, "Oh, they are so happy in there! Surely they will share with me, and let me come into their warm, bright room and sing and play."

And the little feet tripped up the great, wide staircase, and without a fear the child tapped softly at the door.

51

And the door opened.

There stood the tall footman.

He looked at the little child, but sadly shook his head and said: "Go down off the steps. There is no room in here for you." He looked sorry when he said it, for he probably remembered his own little ones at home, and was glad that they were not out in the cold.

Through the open door a light—oh, such a bright light—shone, and it was so warm!

But the child turned away into the cold and darkness, not knowing why the footman spoke so; for surely the children would have loved to have another little companion to join in their joyous Christmas evening festival.

But the children did not know that the child had knocked.

The street seemed colder and darker to the child than before, and the bright windows were not nearly so bright, because the child was sad. But all along, on both sides of the wide street, the light streamed out, and it was almost as bright as day; and the beauty all about made the little child glad again.

The great city was full of happy homes that night, and the cold outside was entirely forgotten. All remembered only the happy time, and no doubt thought that every single person in the whole wide world was happy, too.

Farther and farther along, down where the homes were not quite so large or beautiful, the little child wandered. There seemed to be children inside of nearly all the houses, and they were dancing and frolicking about; there were Christmas-trees in nearly every window, with beautiful dolls and toys; there were trumpets and picture books, and all sorts of nice things; and in one place a sweet little lamb made of white wool was hanging on the tree for one of the children.

The child, stopping before this window,

looked and looked at the beautiful thing, and creeping up to the glass gently tapped upon the pane. A little girl came to the window and looked out into the dark street and saw the child. But she only frowned and shook her head and said, "Come some other time, for we cannot take care of you now," and then she went away.

The little child turned back into the cold again, and went sadly on, saying, "Will no one share the beautiful Christmas with me? The light is so bright and I love it so!" The child wandered on and on, scarcely seeing the light now on account of tears.

The street became darker and narrower; farther and farther the little one traveled. It grew late. Scarcely anyone was out to meet the child as it walked, and all the outer world was still and cold.

Ahead there suddenly appeared a bright, single ray of light, that shone right through the darkness into the child's eyes. The child smiled and said, "I will go and see if they will share their Christmas with me."

Hastening past all the other houses, the little one went straight up to the window-pane from which the light was streaming. It was such a poor, little, low house, but the child saw only the light in the window, for there was neither curtain nor shade. What do you suppose the light came from? Nothing but a tiny tallow candle! But it seemed to the little wanderer almost as bright as the sun. That was because the child was glad again. The candle was placed in an old cup with a broken handle, and right in the same cup there was a twig of evergreen, and that was all the Christmas-tree they had.

And who do you suppose was in the house?

A beautiful mother with a baby on her knee, and a little one beside her. The children were both looking into their mother's face and listening to her words. A few bright coals were burning in the fireplace,

MADONNA AND CHILD
(*Bagman Bouverel*)

which made it light and warm within. The
child crept closer to the window, and gently,
oh, so gently, tapped upon the pane. They
all listened.

"Shall I open the door, dear mother?" the
little girl asked.

"Certainly, my child. No one must be left
out in the cold on our beautiful Christmas eve.
Open the door and let the stranger come in."

The door was thrown wide open and the little girl looked into the darkness; when she
saw the child she put out her little hand to
help. The child went in — into the light and
warmth. Then the mother put out her hands
and touched the little child. The children
said: "Dear little one, you are cold and naked;
come and let us warm you and love you, and
then you shall have some of our Christmas."

The baby crept out of its mother's lap, and
she gathered the little stranger to her, and the
children stood at her knee, and warmed the
cold hands and feet, and rubbed them, and

smoothed the tangled curls, and kissed the child's face; the mother put her arms about the three little ones, and the candle and the firelight shone over them all, and everything was so still.

And the mother's sweet voice spoke in the stillness:

"Little ones," she said, "shall I tell you the *real* Christmas story?"

The children said, "Yes," so the mother began:

"Many, many years ago, this very night, some shepherds were out on the plains watching their sheep. The wee little lambs were asleep, and the large sheep were sleeping, too. The stars shone bright and clear above, and all was very still below.

"The shepherds sat beside each other without a word, leaning on their crooks and hardly moving.

"Suddenly a great light shone all around about them, right through the darkness; they did not know what it was, and they were all afraid.

"Then an angel, white and beautiful, came to them from out the light, and told them not to fear, for great joy and gladness had come to the whole world. A little babe had just been born who was to become their King and save them from all wrong and suffering, and do great good for them and all mankind. The angel then showed the shepherds where to find the babe, saying that it would be wrapped in swaddling clothes and lying in a manger.

"And suddenly there was with the angel a multitude of the heavenly host, praising God and saying, Glory to God in the highest, and on earth peace, good will toward men. And a wonderful light was all about them, and when the angel had gone away from them into heaven, the shepherds said one to another, let us go and see this child of whom the angel told us.

"So they left their lambs sleeping on the

plains, and took their crooks in their hands and started out.

"It was a long way, but a shining star was before them, and they followed it even up to the place where the angel had told them. And they found the babe lying in a manger, and when they had seen it they told all the people that came to see the child of what they had seen that night on the plains, and how the angel had told them to come to the child, and of the wonderful light which had made them afraid; and how the multitude had sung. All they that had heard it wondered at the things which were told them by the shepherds. The mother of the little babe was very glad and remembered all these things.

"The kind shepherds departed and went back to their flocks, telling every one they met of the young child.

"They called the child Jesus, and the child grew, and was strong and beautiful, and Jesus taught the whole world how they should love

ADORATION OF THE SHEPHERDS
(*Bouguereau*)

one another and be good, even as our Father in heaven is good and loves us.''

The sweet voice of the mother ceased. The light in the room had grown brighter, until now it shone like the sun; from the floor to the ceiling all was light as day. And lo, when the little ones turned to look for the child, the mother's lap was empty; there was nothing to be seen; the child was gone but the light was still in the room.

''Children,'' the mother said quietly, ''I believe we have had the real Christ-Child with us to-night.'' And she drew her dear ones to her and kissed them, and there was great joy in the little house.

''*And whoso receiveth one such little child in my name receiveth me.*''

''*For lo! I am with you always.*''

WE all know how sweet were the stories which the boy Jesus read and loved when he was searching, as does every little boy and girl, for happy stories.

Think how much sweeter even must be the stories written about the Christ-Child him-self, and what a wondrous story-teller he must have been who could tell them to the whole world. Of course, in order to write about the Christ-Child in words that would live forever, one would have to know the deepest things in the Christ-heart, and think and feel the same.

The one story-teller who knew Jesus best and loved him most was Saint John. He understood just what Jesus meant when he called God his Father. He knew what Jesus meant when he spoke of heaven, and in the very first story tells of how from the beginning he was with God. There is a beautiful pic-ture of Saint John where he holds the scroll and is all shining with light as he tells of the coming of Christ, when the whole heart world is pure enough to receive him.

In one of his stories he tells of the beautiful city of Love where he lives with the Father and the blessed friends who lived the holy life. This is his last story about the Christ and tells of all his glory and greatness.

The stories easiest to understand are those in which he tells how Jesus took the little children and touched them and loved them; how he gave eyes to the blind and helped them to see; how he walked on the water, fed the people and cured the sick.

John loved to call Jesus the Light, because his heart was full of goodness, and he tells us that it is this true light that lights every man that comes into the world.

This loving friend, Saint John, knew the heart of the Christ-Child as perhaps only his mother knew it, and this is the reason we love his stories about him more than any others.

SAINT JOHN
Domenichino

ALL the year round the three great bells of the village spoke to each other, back and forth from belfry to belfry, nodding and swinging. Each had but one word to say and he said it over and over, asking and answering in the very same tone.

One would throw himself up into the air and hang there, trembling all over — his great tongue quivering — waiting for the answer from his neighbor with the shining brass sides, that hung in the tower across the little stream; and then from far down the valley would peal forth the ring of the third great bell, — all this while the first one was waiting for his turn to speak again.

These bells hung and swung far above the heads of everybody in the village. They had but one thing to say and one way to say it, but since the people did not understand it did very well, and every one loved these three brothers, and never even questioned what they meant.

Though they did not speak in the same tone they were of one mind, and even when they spoke together they did not jangle in the least, but sounded so sweetly — especially in the ears of the children, who always stopped and looked up. Whenever they spoke together thus they told that a little child was born — somewhere in the village some one had a little new brother or sister, and so the children smiled. And when the year was born perhaps that was why the ringing brought them such joy.

"Hark, hark, the bells!"

Every one in the village awoke at twelve o'clock on New Year's Eve except the children, for out on the night there poured the rich clanging of the bells.

All the grown people got up, peered out of the window, saw the clear sky and the ocean of stars, then they wished each other a very sleepy "Happy New Year!" saying that they hoped it would bring some good with it, and back they went to sleep again.

But the children did not wake up—they dreamed on and on under their coverlets; perhaps some of them turned over or stretched themselves, but not a single one opened an eye. Wasn't it strange?

But when the frosty light of the morning poured over the houses from out the blue sky, every single child in the village started out of dreamland, and such dreams as they did tell! From one end of the village to the other every household, where there were any children, heard wonder-tales that could scarcely be believed. They told of having seen flower-beds right out in the snow, and of music and lights all over everything. They told of children with the happiest faces, laughing and playing and dancing and singing, and one little girl awoke in her cradle and found some beautiful flowers had blossomed right out of the dream and were still in her hand. And every one came and marveled over it, and smelled the flowers and knew that they were real. This little one had listened perhaps the best of all to what the dream said, and so the dream came true.

What had come to all the little ones? The wise people of the village were all puzzled, for no one, not even the old sextons who pulled the ropes, had noticed anything strange in the ringing.

There were many old men and women in the village who had heard the bells for years and years, and they did not know as much about their meaning as the little folks, and how they all wondered at the dreams that came to the children on that New Year's night.

This must have been the way it all came about: A beautiful friend who had told the children stories and taught them wonderful things, had asked each to watch for the message of the New Year which comes after the Christ-Child's birth.

Every child that was loving and helpful and trusting would hear on the eve of the New Year a wonder-tale, and don't you see each child went to sleep that night waiting and watching for it, and it had to come. If the grown people had done the same it would probably have come to them, too — but they are often too busy to hear and see even the most beautiful things. We are glad that children are not.

The bells have a really deep story to tell that very few have ever guessed, and what they tell seems easier for the children to understand than for grown folks; it is about the childhood of the year, and how in the beginning, before darkness came over the face of the world, all was beautiful and good and holy.

The song that the New Year sings through the lips of a bell is something like this, if we put it into words that the ears can understand:

> " Good people, awake,
> And list to the bell:—
> Begin with the year
> To know that all's well."

Listen! and perhaps on New Year's Eve each one of us may hear the happiest greeting, so that the next day when we call out a "glad New Year" to every friend we meet, there will be so much joy in it that they will be gladder than they ever were before.

MADONNA AND CHILD, WITH WREATH
(*Rubens*)

A Flower Carol.

"AWAKE, awake, my buds of white!"
    The mother primrose said,
    "Lift up each dainty head!
And with your petals pure, uncurled,
Sing of the Christ-Child, born to-night
    Into a frozen world!"

Each snowy blossom started up
    From its sweet budding sleep,
    And one by one began to creep
From out the primrose mother's lap;
And gently every flower cup
    Unfolded from its nap.

And opening wide their sweet lips white
    The primrose children told,
    From out their hearts of gold,
The story of the child so dear—
The child that came on Christmas night—
    The child that still is here.

The only words the flowers had
    With which to sing their song—
    So full and sweet and strong—
  Were precious scents of rich perfume;
And from their fresh-blown petals glad,
  It rose and filled the room.

A-RING-A-RING, ring! A-ring-a-ring, ring!

"Brother Carl, wake up! wake up! Don't you hear the great bell? Father is ringing the New Year in, don't you hear it, little Carl? Wake up!"

Tangled-haired little Carl sat up in bed, rubbed his eyes, and after a few winks opened them wide.

"Is it the wind, brother Hans, that sings so?"

"No, no! It is the great bell; don't you hear it ring? It is ringing for the New Year."

"Is father drawing the rope?" asked the little one.

"Of course he is, little Carl; he is waking up the whole world that every one may wish a 'Happy New Year.' Come, let us go to the window."

And the two little fellows crept out of their

warm nest onto the cold floor, and over to the window in the gable.

"Oh, see, there is father's lantern in the steeple window!" cried Carl.

It threw its light into the frosty night; the clear stars cut sharp holes in the sky, and the air was so cold it made everything glisten.

A-ring-a-ring, ring! clanged the great bell, and little Hans and Carl knew that father's arms were making it ring. The strokes were so strong that each one made little half-asleep Carl wink; and the stars seemed to wink back to him each time. He crept closer to Hans, and the two stood still with their arms about each other; the room was quite cold, but they did not mind it, for with each stroke the great bell seemed to ring more beautifully. It seemed so near them, as if ringing right in their ears, and the two little boys stood and listened with beating hearts.

"I saw dear father fix his lantern," whispered Hans. "He set it near the door before we went to bed, all ready to light when the clock struck twelve. Mother said to him as he put the lantern there, 'Ring the bell good and strong, dear father, for who knows but this year may bring the great blessing which the Christ-Child promised!' We must watch for it, little Carl."

And the old bell seemed to speak louder and clearer to the little ones, as they eagerly listened for what it was telling.

"Father says the bell will never ring from the old tower again for the new one is being built," said Hans. "And what do you think, brother Carl, our dear mother wept because the old steeple must be broken down, and the dear bell, that is even now a-ringing, must be put into another great tower to ring."

"Does the great bell know it, brother?"

"No, dear little Carl; but no matter where it is put it will always ring, and be glad to wake the village for the New Year."

"Will we go and say good-bye to the dear

old bell, brother Hans?" whispered little Carl.

"Yes, dear brother mine; when it is day we will go, for it has rung so many times for us."

They crept out of the cold into their snug bed again, and the great strokes poured from the tower window long after the little curly heads were full of dreams.

"Wake up, brother Hans! there is the sun." This time little Carl was the first to arise. Quickly they were both dressed, and opening their door noiselessly they went down the narrow stairs on tiptoe, and then out into the open air.

A swift wind was blowing. It swept over the bare bushes and whirled the snow into the children's faces, and filled their curly hair with flakes. But the sun was smiling down on them and said, "See what a beautiful day I brought for a New Year's gift to you!"

And the little ones passed through the church door, that was always open, and into the belfry tower. They knew the way, for father had so often taken them with him.

They came to the long, dark ladder-way; but they did not mind the dark—for they knew the bell was at the top, and they bravely began to climb.

Hans had wooden shoes, so he left them at the foot of the ladder. It is so much easier to climb a ladder with bare feet. Besides, he hardly felt the cold he was such a quick and lively little boy.

Carl went ahead that brother Hans might the more easily help him. They climbed, up and up, and the brave big brother talked merrily all the time, to keep little Carl from thinking of the long, long way. Up and up they went. It became darker and darker. Little Carl led on and on, and he was glad that Hans was behind him.

All at once a bright stream of light greeted them from above, and they knew that soon they would be with the dear old bell.

75

Through the opening they crept, and there the great bell hung and they stood beneath it. Hans could just touch it, and he felt of its long tongue and saw the shining marks of its sides where it had struck in clanging for many, many years.

It was very cold in the belfry. Little Carl tucked his hands under his blouse and gazed at the bell, while Hans explained to him what made the music, and the great tolling tones came from it.

"The whole world loves the great bell, brother Carl," said Hans. "Mother thinks that last night it rang in the great blessing which the Christ-Child had promised."

"What did the little Christ-Child promise, brother?"

"Don't you remember, little Carl? Mother told us that the Christ-Child would send little children a beautiful gift; I think it must be the New Year that he has sent, for that is what the old bell brought to us last night."

MADONNA OF THE WAISTBAND
(*Murillo*)

And Hans lifted little Carl, and he kissed the beautiful bell on its great round lip, and the bell was still warm from its long ringing.

And they stood and looked at the bell quietly for a long time. And then they said, "Good-bye, dear great bell," and they went down the long, dark ladder again.

Hans put on his wooden shoes at the foot of the ladder, and with flying feet they crossed the church garden, and there stood the dear mother in the door looking for them. She had found their little bed empty, and was just starting out to find them.

"Dear mother, we have been in the tower to thank the great bell for bringing the New Year," cried Hans.

"Did the Christ-Child send it, mother?" asked little Carl.

The mother stooped and put her arms about them and kissed them both. As she led them into the room she said, "Yes, my little ones, the Christ-Child sends the New Year."

TWELVE little sleepy boys, rubbing their eyes and stretching their mouths as wide as ever they could with yawns, were standing in the snow, waiting.

They were right under the window of their dear old godfather's house, and it was early Christmas morning, long before daylight.

Suddenly, out on the frosty air their voices spoke, chiming so sweetly that the dear god-father must certainly have thought he was dreaming of angels as he waked.

Upstairs, inside the house, in his own little bedroom, and on his own old-fashioned bed, the old man lay. Suddenly he sat up, brushed his nightcap away from his ears, and this is what he heard:

"Carol, brothers, carol,
   Carol joyfully;
 Carol the good tidings,
   Carol merrily.

Carol but in gladness,
  Not in songs of earth,
On the Saviour's birthday
  Hallowed be our mirth."

And the dear godfather wiped away a tear, for he knew that these little lads must surely love him, if they would creep out of their trundle beds so early on a cold morning to remind him of the Christ-Child and his coming.

The good old man crept out of his warm bed to go to the window. Just then the singer began the second verse:

"While the heavens are telling
  To mankind good-will,
Only love and kindness
  Every bosom fill.

And pray a gladsome Christmas
  For all good Christian men,
Carol, brothers, carol,
  Christmas day again."

He threw open the window wide, and called to his little godchildren, and they came into the large hall and warmed themselves by the fireplace. He gave them raisins and cakes to eat, for they had not had any breakfast.

Then by the candle-light the godfather showed them beautiful pictures of the Christ-Child and its lovely mother. He told them how Jesus loved the world and served the poor and sick.

And there in the fire-light the boys sang their sweet songs over and over for him, and when the beautiful Christmas morning broke over the village, the godfather kissed each rosy face and sent his beloved godchildren with gifts in their hands to go to the poor and old to wake them with their joyful songs of Christ's birth.

HOLY FAMILY
(*Knaus*)

Christmas Wreaths.

OH let us wind the holly
 In Christmas garlands gay,
It lives so long, and glistens
 When roses fade away!

Wind it on the stairs and windows
 And on the cradles, too—
The babies love the holly
 Quite as much as you.

Christmas was made for babies,
 All their own to keep;
It's the birthday of that Baby
 Who was cradled with the sheep.

Here's holly for the babies!
 And on their cribs upstairs
We'll weave its branches, green and
   red,
 For Christmas day is theirs.

EVEN after the Christ-Child had come upon the earth, and the children of the world and the grown people, too, had heard the story over and over, they still watched and waited for him.

When he went to his Father, his last words had been promises of his coming back again, and sweet thoughts like these he left with us: I go to my Father, but I shall return again; Lo, I am with you alway. So it is no wonder that the world went on waiting and watching, and working to be good enough to receive him when he came again.

Far back, many years ago, when good men were called saints, there lived one named Christopher. He was very large and strong, and could lift the heaviest burdens on his back, and his legs were so stout that he could travel far without growing tired.

Although he loved God and did all the

good things he could, yet he knew very little
of the wise things of the world, and thought
it would be almost useless for him to think
of serving the King of Heaven by prayers
and beautiful words, as did all the people who
passed through his home place on their way
to Jerusalem.

One day he went to a very good brother
who was wiser than many others, and who
lived all alone in a cave and was called a hermit. He thought he would ask him what
he might do to serve God more and better
than he had ever before. The hermit lived
a long way, so Christopher broke off a palm-
tree to use as a staff, for he was a man of
great power.

When he found the hermit, he said to him:
"Brother, I am strong and large; I can bear
heavy loads and walk through stony paths
long distances and never weary. See this
palm which I broke with my single hand.
Yet, brother, I would rather serve God and

have his blessing than be strong without a purpose."

"Then, good Christopher, you may do as I tell you. There is a river with a stony bottom, wide and deep, with steep banks, through which all our people must pass on their way to Jerusalem. There is no bridge nor any other path, and every rain fills these high banks, and many people are compelled to wait and lose their way. Do you know the river?"

Christopher bowed his head.

"If you would serve God, go and serve his people, and help them over this water, so deep and rocky and wide."

Christopher bowed his head again.

"Why do you not speak? Do you fear?" the hermit asked.

But Christopher only raised his head and answered: "It is nothing for me to carry loads and fight the water. I want to learn beautiful prayers and go as a pilgrim with the other worshipers."

84

"Christopher, my brother," said the hermit, "serve and love your brethren first, and then you will begin to know how to serve and love the Father. You will know, some day, why I speak thus; for when you love others you love the Christ-Child as well."

And Christopher bowed his head and went away. He took his great staff, made of the palm-tree which he had torn up, and with other palms he built himself a hut at the crossing of the river. There day after day he toiled and helped the travelers over. When the rains came and the water was very deep he would put people on his shoulders, and when little children came to cross, he always bore them so much more joyously.

At night the people would call out to him, and if there was not a single star he would go just the same, without a question; for his brave feet knew every stone in the watery path.

One very dark night — so dark that Christopher almost prayed that no one would come to call him out into the rain—he heard a cry, as if a baby were without its mother in the storm.

"It is the wind," said Christopher; and he tried to sleep and forget.

Again the cry came: "Christopher, come, come!"

He raised his head, threw about him his coat, and opened the door. His light flickered out, and the storm still roared.

"Christopher, Christopher, come and carry me over!" And he broke through the door and went out into the dark.

There in the storm he found a young child, naked and all alone, sitting and waiting for him.

"Carry me over, good Christopher. I must go to-night, for I promised so many beyond here that I was coming, and they are waiting and watching for me. Carry me over, good Christopher!"

SAINT CHRISTOPHER AND CHRIST-CHILD
(*Titian*)

Christopher looked down upon the dear child; he smiled and lifted him to his strong shoulders, and taking up his staff he stepped into the swollen stream. The waters rushed about them. The great stones in the bottom had been moved from their places, but Christopher walked carefully, and the little one clung to him so tightly that he had no fear.

As he stepped out deeper and deeper into the river his burden seemed to grow heavier and heavier, for the water beat against them both.

It seemed as though they must surely sink, for it was a wild, wild night.

Each step was harder than the last, and his breath came hard, and his knees could scarcely hold out any longer, so heavy had his burden grown. His palm staff bent as it helped him along, and the river seemed never so wide before.

At length he touched the other side safe and weary. He set the child down; gently and lovingly he did it, with never a thought of how hard he had worked to help. And suddenly, as the clouds broke and the moonlight fell upon them, he saw a beautiful being with shining face and holy smile; and in the quiet of the night he broke out with — "Who are you, my child? who are you? for had I carried the whole world on my shoulders to serve God it could not have been harder. Tell me who you are."

And the sweet voice said: "Good Christopher, I am he who has promised to come to you, and whom you have been serving. Did you not know that in this humble, hard work at serving all, you were serving me and the Father? With whatever strength you have you shall serve, and it shall all be holy. Your staff, too, has served with all its power. If you will plant it in the ground you shall see what beautiful things live even in a dry staff when it works for others."

Christopher did so, and suddenly it blossomed into a beautiful fresh palm-tree, full of fruit. And his great heart was filled with content, for he knew that he and his staff had served the Christ-Child.

And the Christ passed on into the early morning light that was breaking.

Down the long pathway he went, on and on, to cheer the waiting people all the way.

And Christopher went back to his holy work of serving men; and he no longer needed his staff, for his happy heart never let him lose courage since he knew he was serving the Christ-Child.

JESUS always remembered the beautiful days of his childhood, for in his heart he was always young. He loved little children because they knew how to love better than anyone else. As he watched them playing about him, singing and frolicking with each other, he would say: "They are of my Father's house; they are of the kingdom of heaven because they know what pure joy is."

Whenever there were any children about he would call them to him and they would fly to his loving arms, and the mothers would bring their babies for him to touch and kiss, for they felt that he loved them even more than they, for he knew so well how to love.

What did he see when he looked into the sweet face of a child?

Yes, he saw back of the eyes, deep down in the heart, the pure child of God which dwells in each one of us, and he told all the people

CHRIST BLESSING LITTLE CHILDREN
(*Plockhurst*)

that they must become again as this beautiful
child before they would know what the kingdom of heaven was; and when they kept their
hearts pure as a little child they would know
God and dwell with him.

He taught every one of us to look into each
others' eyes and seek the pure child of God
there. Think, if we did this always! We
would find all our friends in the heaven within, and then we would have the kingdom of
heaven without and all about us. He told us
we must do this when he taught us to pray:
"Thy kingdom come on earth."

Each one of us must do his share to help it
to come.